D0535415

J. MORIA STEPHENS

Persephone
the Ladybug

Little, Brown and Company

Boston New York London

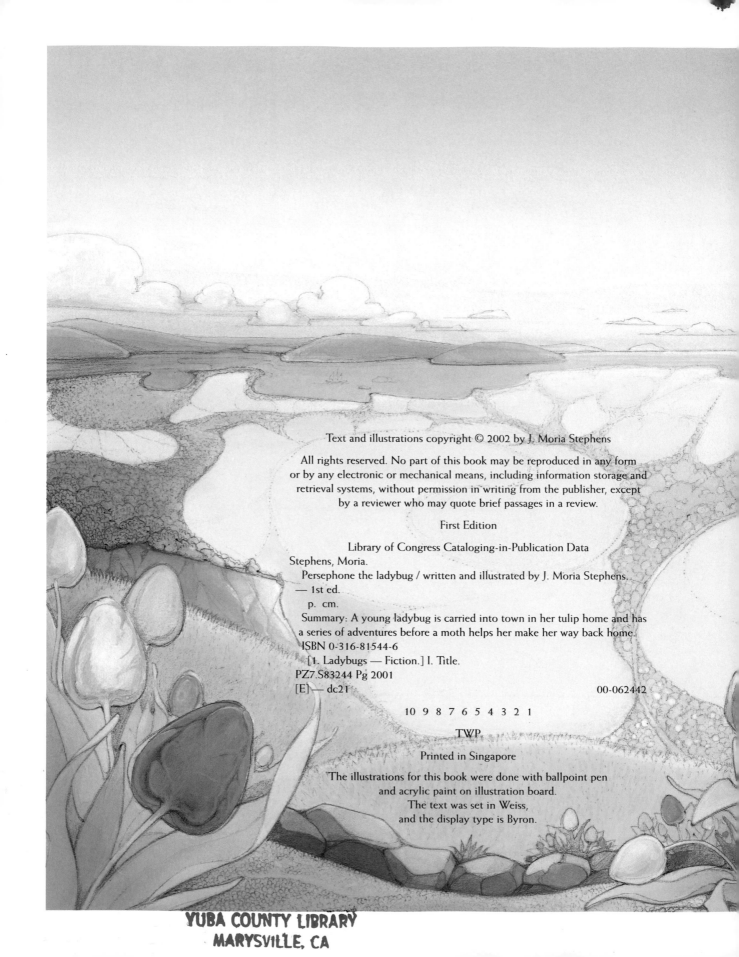

First Edition

Library of Congress Cataloging-in-Publication Data
Stephens, Moria.
  Persephone the ladybug / written and illustrated by J. Moria Stephens.
  — 1st ed.
    p. cm.
  Summary: A young ladybug is carried into town in her tulip home and has
a series of adventures before a moth helps her make her way back home.
  ISBN 0-316-81544-6
  [1. Ladybugs — Fiction.] I. Title.
PZ7.S83244 Pg 2001
[E] — dc21   00-062442

10 9 8 7 6 5 4 3 2 1

TWP

Printed in Singapore

The illustrations for this book were done with ballpoint pen
and acrylic paint on illustration board.
The text was set in Weiss,
and the display type is Byron.

For Mum and Dad, with love and gratitude for
years of encouragement and support.

And to Shelli, whose perseverance despite adversity
inspired the character of Persephone.

Persephone lived with her mother in a tulip in East Bugfield Village. Every day, her mother would go out to work, but Persephone would stay home. She was still too small to go to school with all the other bug children, so she made herself useful doing little household chores. She swept and scrubbed and dusted and polished. Once her home was gleaming, Persephone sat down to rest and wait for her mother to return.

Every evening, Persephone would implore her mother to give her flying
lessons. "You're still too young, my dear," her mother would always reply.
"When a crescent moon is in the sky and summer heat is on the land,
then it will be time for you to fly." Persephone grew more impatient every
day, but she had to wait.

One morning while her mother was out, Persephone was sweeping up some loose pollen when she was suddenly thrown across the room. In an instant the floor tilted wildly and she found herself being tossed about. Dizzy and frightened, Persephone curled up tightly into a ball and waited for the motion to stop.

What could it possibly be? A windstorm? A woodland animal out for a
stroll? Far worse! East Bugfield Village was under attack! Before the hour
was out, every last tulip had been cut down and loaded into a pony cart,
bound for Starchester Flower Market in Big City.

The next day, Persephone awoke worried and confused. Her mother still had not returned, nor could she hear the sounds of busy bugs and birds that usually accompanied her mornings. To make matters worse, her home was badly damaged and through its thin walls came the faint din of foreign voices.

As time passed, the spaces in the tulip's walls and ceilings grew into large gaps. The petals began to drop off one by one until Persephone found herself clinging to the stem of her old home, surrounded by a strange, new world with a hard, flat ground far below.

Persephone was immediately put to work at the back of the kitchen, where she was adept at handling small chores. Of course she and the humans who surrounded her could not speak the same language, but she understood well enough what tasks needed doing. She scoured fork tines, polished small fruit, and made tea bags by stuffing cloth envelopes with fragrant herbs.

As the days passed by, Persephone became accustomed to her new life. She proved helpful as she removed slugs from the strawberry plants, counted currants for the currant buns, and chased down soap bubbles during the washing up. For a while, the tea shop staff doted on Persephone and found her efforts charming and helpful.

But all too quickly, the novelty of having a pet ladybug wore off. The murmurs of praise Persephone had grown accustomed to were soon only a distant memory, and she felt lonely, neglected, and homesick.

At the end of each day, Persephone was given a few cake crumbs for dinner. After picnicking in the window boxes, she journeyed back across the kitchen to her cozy corner of the linen cupboard. There she would dream of flying home to her mother and the happy life she had known.

One particularly beautiful evening, after the shop had closed, Persephone lingered by the window to watch the stars come out. At last a chilly breeze interrupted her reverie. She turned to go, but was alarmed to discover that darkness had swallowed up every last scrap of daylight in the tea shop. Cold and more than a bit frightened, Persephone set off running as fast as she could back to the safety of the linen cupboard.

In the inky blackness, Persephone lost her way several times. She tripped over a teaspoon, knocked into the sugar bowl, and almost fell off the countertop. Scared and breathless, she finally rounded the last corner, then recoiled in horror. . . .

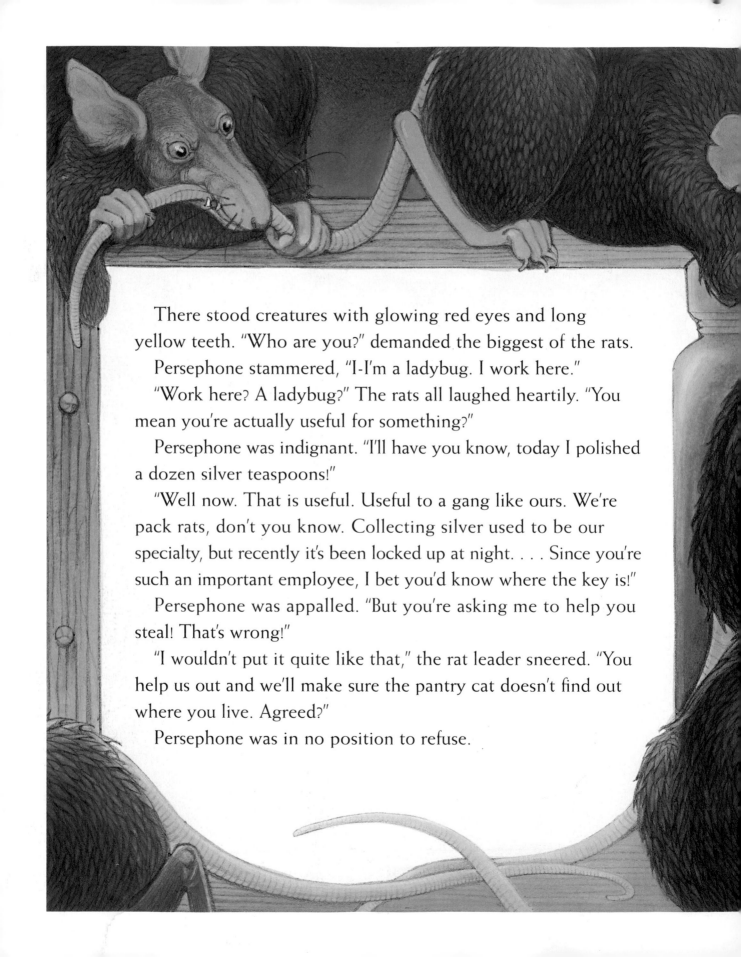

There stood creatures with glowing red eyes and long yellow teeth. "Who are you?" demanded the biggest of the rats.

Persephone stammered, "I-I'm a ladybug. I work here."

"Work here? A ladybug?" The rats all laughed heartily. "You mean you're actually useful for something?"

Persephone was indignant. "I'll have you know, today I polished a dozen silver teaspoons!"

"Well now. That is useful. Useful to a gang like ours. We're pack rats, don't you know. Collecting silver used to be our specialty, but recently it's been locked up at night. . . . Since you're such an important employee, I bet you'd know where the key is!"

Persephone was appalled. "But you're asking me to help you steal! That's wrong!"

"I wouldn't put it quite like that," the rat leader sneered. "You help us out and we'll make sure the pantry cat doesn't find out where you live. Agreed?"

Persephone was in no position to refuse.

The next day, Persephone began the dreadful task of helping the rats.
Just before closing time, when all the other help were bustling about
putting on coats and thinking about their lives outside the tea shop, she
took a small key and quickly unlocked the silver drawer.

After she had replaced the key, Persephone watched in horror as the Pack Rat Gang swarmed through the silver drawers. What would her mother think, Persephone wondered, if she knew her daughter had become no better than a common thief? She felt so guilty about what she had done that she couldn't sleep a wink that night.

HERBERT'S
FANCY SMALL
PICKLES

VERY
OLD
GOURMET
COOKING
WINE

GOOSEBERRY
RELISH

The following afternoon, Persephone set about the task of polishing water spots off a freshly washed teacup. She was very tired. The cup was warm and smelled faintly of lemon soap. Persephone polished slower and slower, until finally she wasn't polishing at all but snoozing soundly at the bottom of the cup.

During the teatime bustle, Starchester's waitresses hurriedly delivered heavily laden tea trays and trolleys. Persephone was entirely forgotten about. . . . That is, until Starchester's most important patrons were served a sleeping bug with their tea. Persephone was abruptly awoken by the shrieks and gasps of the horrified tea takers.

Mr. Parsnip was furious. He held Persephone aloft above ruined cakes, overturned teapots, and broken china. "This is intolerable! A bug in the tea! And more silverware gone missing, as well! What will people think of the Starchester Tea Shop now?"

"You stay here and think about what you've done. No
crumbs for dinner tonight, Miss Ladybug! We'll decide what's
to be done with you tomorrow."

Persephone was so dejected that she didn't notice as the
shop closed up for the day and dusk silently approached. She
had entirely forgotten that before long the rats would swarm
through the kitchen in search of more loot.

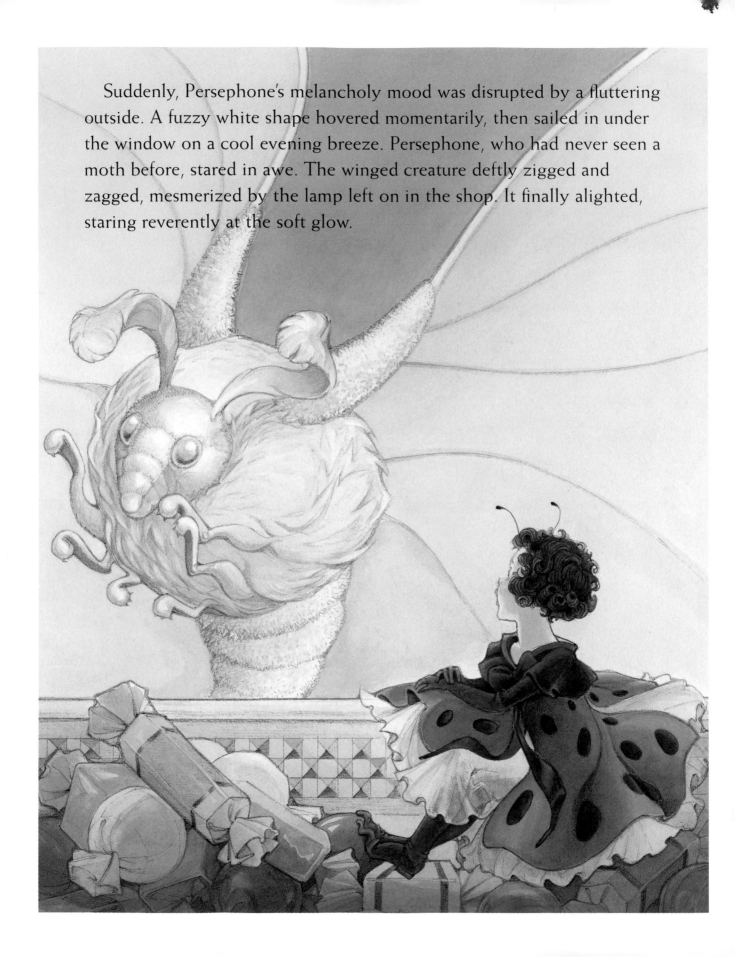

Suddenly, Persephone's melancholy mood was disrupted by a fluttering outside. A fuzzy white shape hovered momentarily, then sailed in under the window on a cool evening breeze. Persephone, who had never seen a moth before, stared in awe. The winged creature deftly zigged and zagged, mesmerized by the lamp left on in the shop. It finally alighted, staring reverently at the soft glow.

Then Persephone heard the sound she dreaded—the scurry and clamor
of the Pack Rat Gang as they raced from darkened corners toward the
silver drawer. When they found it locked, the rat leader cursed angrily,
looked around, and then spotted Persephone on her perch.

"Hey, I thought we had a deal!" he yelled. "Biff, Bob, get that bug.
We'll feed her to the cat along with her new fluffy friend!"

"Please, help me!" called Persephone to the moth. But the moth continued
to stare at the lamp and did not respond.

Like an inky wave, the rats rushed toward the two helpless creatures, overtaking them from all sides. Persephone's perch was overturned, and she and the moth were thrown together in a jumble. They clung to each other in fear. But the rats, in their haste, carelessly knocked over the lamp. The room suddenly went pitch black. The only light now came from a thin crescent moon outside. Free of the lamp's enchantment, the moth snapped out of its strange spell and began to rise into the night. Persephone, still clinging to it, felt the ground drop swiftly from beneath her feet.

The moth moved unerringly toward the open window as the rats lunged and leaped to grab them. But in another moment, Persephone found herself bathed in fragrant spring air. The Starchester Tea Shop grew smaller and smaller below them, and the sounds of vengeful rats dwindled into the hush of the quiet street.

For the rest of that night, the moth flew, guided by the crescent moon. At dawn, the moon paled and faded into the sky and the moth flew onward toward sunrise.

In the distance, Persephone thought she could see bright fields dotted with flowers. "Oh, look!" she cried out ecstatically. "I think we're heading home."

An encouraging breeze sent them sailing toward the horizon.